Library of Congress Cataloging-in-Publication Data:
George, Barbara. The Wuzzles' fair. SUMMARY: Tony, unable to go to the fair because he is recovering from chicken pox, is transported to the Land of Wuz to enjoy the fair put on by the Wuzzles. [1. Fairs—Fiction. 2. Chicken pox—Fiction] I. Duell, Nancy, ill. II. Title. PZ7.G29314Wu 1986 [E] 85-18357 ISBN: 0-394-87912-0

Manufactured in the United States of America   1 2 3 4 5 6 7 8 9 0

The Wuzzles' Fair

by Barbara George
illustrated by Nancy Duell

RANDOM HOUSE NEW YORK

In the Land of Wuz the Wuzzles were having a
quiet picnic lunch of spaghetti and pickle
sandwiches with tomato-berry tea.

Eleroo was lazily flipping through a magazine
he had found in his pocket. "Say, gang! Take a
look at this!"

"Wow! The Supercolossal Traveling Fair looks like fun!" said Rhinokey.

"I guess it won't ever come here," Butterbear said sadly.

"But that doesn't mean we can't have our own fair," said Moosel. "I'll bet we could build rides like those!"

And that's just what the Wuzzles decided to do!

Far, far away, a boy named Tony was sick in bed with itchy chicken pox.

And to make things even worse, the Supercolossal Traveling Fair was coming to town in just a week.

"Oh, Bumblelion," said Tony as he snuzzled his soft toy Wuzzle. "I have to be well enough to go to the fair. I just *have* to be!"

While Tony was doing his best to get better
and trying hard not to scratch, the Wuzzles were
hard at work in the Land of Wuz.

"Our rides won't be exactly like the pictures,"
said Moosel.

"They'll be better!" said Hoppopotamus.

"It's good I keep things," said Eleroo.

There weren't any merry-go-round horses in Eleroo's pocket, but he found lots of leaky hoses, broken bicycles, and a music box that played "Pop Goes the Wuzzle!"

"With a little work we can build a merry-get-wet," said Eleroo.

"And I'll run it," said Bumblelion.

"My pocket has never felt so empty," said Eleroo.

"Well, I hope you have a crystal ball in there," said Hoppopotamus. "I'm going to be a gypsy who tells fortunes."

"And I'm going to sell pop-berry-corn," said Butterbear.

Meanwhile, the Supercolossal Traveling Fair had arrived in town for just three days.

What excitement! Tony knew that all of his friends were going. But even though his chicken pox had faded to pink dots, his parents said he wasn't quite well enough to go. And no amount of begging would change their minds.

"Oh, Bumblelion!" Tony whispered in the darkness. "I wish I could go to the fair. I wish, I just wish!"

And then something very strange happened. One moment Tony was in his very own bed in his very own room and the next moment...

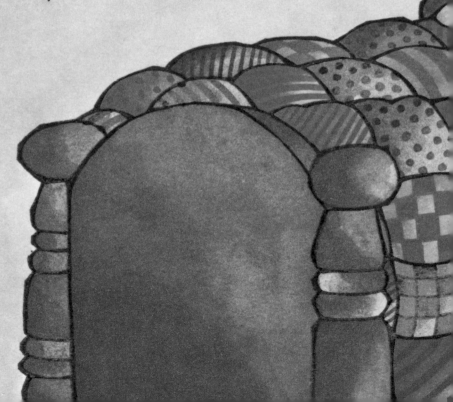

He was in the Land of Wuz! And the real Bumblelion was saying, "Welcome to the Wuzzles' Fair!"

Tony loved the rides, and he thought Butterbear's
pop-berry-corn tasted better than cotton candy.

"I see many fairs in your future," said
Hoppopotamus.

The Supercolossal Traveling Fair still visits Tony's town, and Tony still goes.

But even though it's supposed to be bigger and better every year, Tony thinks the Wuzzles' Fair is the most wonderful fair—the very best fair—that ever wuz…or could be.